The Five Little Peppers and How They Grew

Retold from the Margaret Sidney
original by Diane Namm

Illustrated by Dan Andreasen

STERLING

New York / London
www.sterlingpublishing.com/kids

STERLING and the distinctive Sterling logo
are registered trademarks of Sterling Publishing Co., Inc.

Library of Congress Cataloging-in-Publication Data

Namm, Diane.
 The five little Peppers and how they grew / retold from the Margaret Sidney original ;
abridged by Diane Namm ; illustrated by Dan Andreasen.
    p. cm. — (Classic starts)
 Summary: An abridged retelling of the Margaret Sidney story in which a fatherless
family, happy in spite of its impoverished condition, is befriended by a very rich
gentleman.
 ISBN-13: 978-1-4027-5420-3
 ISBN-10: 1-4027-5420-5
 [1. Family life—New England—Fiction. 2. Brothers and sisters—Fiction.
3. Poverty—Fiction. 4. Single-parent families—Fiction. 5. New England—History—
19th century—Fiction.] I. Andreasen, Dan, ill. II. Sidney, Margaret,
1844–1924. Five little Peppers and how they grew. III. Title.
 PZ7.N14265Fiv 2009
 [Fic]—dc22

                                                                                2008001966

2 4 6 8 10 9 7 5 3 1

Published by Sterling Publishing Co., Inc.
387 Park Avenue South, New York, NY 10016
Text copyright © 2009 by Diane Namm
Illustrations copyright © 2009 by Dan Andreasen
Distributed in Canada by Sterling Publishing
c/o Canadian Manda Group, 165 Dufferin Street,
Toronto, Ontario, Canada M6K 3H6
Distributed in the United Kingdom by GMC Distribution Services,
Castle Place, 166 High Street, Lewes, East Sussex, England BN7 1XU
Distributed in Australia by Capricorn Link (Australia) Pty. Ltd.
P.O. Box 704, Windsor, NSW 2756, Australia

Classic Starts is a trademark of Sterling Publishing Co., Inc.

Printed in China
All rights reserved

Sterling ISBN 978-1-4027-5420-3

For information about custom editions, special sales, premium and
corporate purchases, please contact Sterling Special Sales
Department at 800-805-5489 or specialsales@sterlingpublishing.com.

CONTENTS

⤔

CHAPTER 1

Happy Days at the Little Brown House

⌒∽

Long, long ago, in a small village known as Badgertown, on a tiny street called Promise Lane, there was a Little Brown House in which the Pepper Family lived.

There was Mrs. Pepper, who was always bent over her sewing in order to earn the money to feed her large brood of five Peppers. Her children called her Mamsie.

Ben, the oldest Pepper child, was eleven years old. He worked hard at Deacon Blodgett's and did all the outdoor chores around the Little Brown House.

Polly, second oldest, was ten years old. She did all the baking, cooking, and cleaning up. And, she took care of Joel, Davie, and Phronsie, so that Mamsie could sew.

By evening, the old kitchen in the Little Brown House was finally quiet. Gone was the hustle and bustle of the day. All of the Peppers, except for Ben, were busy doing small chores.

Life was hard for the Peppers. Mr. Pepper had died when the youngest, Phronsie, was just a baby. Since then, Mrs. Pepper had worked hard to scrape together enough money to buy food and pay rent on the Little Brown House. Day after day, she worked cheerfully at her sewing. She made coats and did mending of all kinds.

In spite of it all, the five little Peppers were a happy bunch and filled Mrs. Pepper's heart with joy. There was only one thing missing: The

Peppers had never been to school. There were so many chores and so little money, that the children had to help as best they could, every day.

"I must get schooling for them somehow. I must," Mrs. Pepper promised herself as her fingers flew over the coat she was sewing.

"To help Mother" was the greatest goal of each and every Pepper. Ben and Polly spent hours making secret plans, whispering to each other about how they would one day surprise Mother with all the kind things they would do for her.

The younger three Peppers, Joel, Davie, and Phronsie, looked up to and loved Polly and Ben with all their hearts. The Peppers felt they were a very lucky family, indeed. They might not have much money, but they had each other, and that was all that really mattered.

"Oh my goodness," said Polly as she burst into the kitchen. "It's almost dinnertime. Ben will be home from work any minute!"

Polly reached into the potato sack that hung in the mostly empty cupboard. She pulled out six potatoes, one for each of them.

"I'll help you, dear, just as soon as I'm done with this mending," Mrs. Pepper said.

"I want to help, too," sang out Phronsie, who toddled in on her chubby little legs and clung to Polly. "May I, Polly? May I?"

"Of course you may, my pet," Polly told her, kissing the top of Phronsie's golden head. Polly set Phronsie down on a seat at the table and gave her a crust of bread and butter.

"You don't need to do a thing, Mamsie," Polly said cheerily to her mother. "Phronsie and I will take care of it all."

Polly hummed as she set a pot of water to boil on the cranky, old black stove. Her brown eyes twinkled in the dimming light as she peeled the potatoes, cut up the brown bread, and set out the butter plate on the old plank-wood table.

"Someday, we'll have enough candles to light the whole house every night," Polly promised herself as she watched Mamsie squint at her sewing in the growing dark.

Just then, Phronsie let out a cry.

"It's Ben!"

Ben bounded into the kitchen, his chubby face all-aglow. His big, blue eyes shone honest and true.

"Is supper ready, Polly?" Ben asked.

"We're hungry," said Joel and Davie, who trailed in after Ben.

"Let's eat!" Polly said, carrying the plate of potatoes to the table.

"Someday, we're going to be awfully rich, aren't we Ben?" Phronsie asked, her mouth half-full.

"You don't say," Ben said with a chuckle. Then in a low voice to Polly he added, "I wish we could be rich now, in time for Mamsie's birthday."

"I know," said Polly sadly. "If only we could really celebrate it."

"I don't want any other celebration than to look at all of you. I feel perfectly rich right now, and that's a fact!" Mrs. Pepper said. Her bright, eyes glistened with pride. "If we can only keep together, dears, and grow up good. That's all I ask," she added.

After dinner, when all the dishes had been washed and neatly put away, Polly said in a low voice, "Ben, we must have a birthday surprise for Mamsie. We simply must!"

"How, Polly?" asked Ben.

Polly wrinkled her forehead and thought a moment.

"Oh, I know. I'll bake her a cake!" Polly said in delight.

"She will see you bake it," said Ben, who was always very practical. "Or, she'll smell it, and that would be just as bad."

"She won't," said Polly. "Mamsie is going to help Mrs. Henderson tomorrow. So, I can bake it then, and we can hide it for the next day's surprise. So there!"

"Good for you, Polly," said Ben. "You always think of everything!"

"We'll have it all done and out of the way by the time Mamsie comes home," Polly said, checking the cupboard. "Oh dear, we've only got brown flour. No matter. Grandma Bascom will tell me how to bake a brown flour cake. I'm going to go right over there and ask her."

"Wait, Polly," said Ben, and he stopped her from flying off right then and there. "Mamsie will find out if you leave now. And, what if the stove stops working the way it always does. What will we do then, Polly?" Ben asked.

Polly ran over and shook her fist at the mean, old face of the crumbling black stove. "I will shake it to pieces!" Polly said so fiercely that Ben had to laugh.

The sound of Ben's laughter brought in all the other children. Ben and Polly told them about the secret birthday cake that Polly was going to bake. The children were so excited that they all stayed up way past their bedtime. Phronsie, who sat straight up on her little stool, blinked and winked to try to stay awake, until finally she tumbled over in a sleepy little heap onto the floor.

"I want to go to bed, Polly. Take me," Phronsie murmured.

So, Polly bundled Phronsie into bed.

And, all the little Peppers dreamed happily of cake and icing and Mamsie's birthday surprise.

∽

The next morning, Polly surveyed the neat little kitchen with pride. The floors were neatly swept, the dishes done, and everything was in order. She and the rest of the little Peppers had gotten up extra-early to finish the morning chores. Ben gave Polly a secret wink as he went to work at Deacon Blodgett's.

The minute Mamsie left, Polly and the three youngest Peppers gathered around the old stove to light it. That way it would be nice and hot to bake the cake.

Davie brought the wood for stove. Polly put it into the stove and poked it into a careful little pile.

"There, that will work!" Polly exclaimed.

Then she saw the big black hole in the back of the stove. The clay that Ben had used to fill the hole had fallen out.

"What will we do, now?" groaned Joel.

"We'll fill it with paper," Polly said.

"We don't have any," said Joel. "We used the last bit of paper to make kites."

"And the kites blew away and got torn to shreds on a tree," Davie added.

"Now we can't have cake!" Joel cried.

"No cake?" asked Phronsie. Her eyes filled with tears and her lip began to tremble.

Davie ran into his room. Two seconds later, he returned with the top of a leather boot he'd found in the road. It was one of his greatest treasures. "We can cram it into the hole as hard as we can," he said.

Polly's eyes shone. "You're a real good boy, Davie, to let us use this," she said, giving Davie a hug.

"I would have given a boot-top if I'd had one," Joel said.

"I know, Joel," Polly said kindly and gave him a quick hug.

Polly bent down beside the stove and poked at the fire. Soon, it began to burn. Then she stood up, wiped her hands on her apron, and drew a long relieved breath.

"I'm going to Grandma Bascom's to get a recipe for birthday cake," Polly said. "You boys stay here and take care of Phronsie and the house."

"I've got lots of hammering to do," Joel said, puffing his chest up proudly.

Polly kissed the three littlest Peppers goodbye and set off for Grandma Bascom's house.

Grandma Bascom wasn't really Polly's grandmother, but everyone in the village called her that. Polly flew across the lane, around the corner, and right through Grandma Bascom's front door. There was no point in knocking. Grandma couldn't hear much of anything at all.

"Good morning, Polly, dear," Grandma welcomed her. "How's your mother?" she asked.

"It's her birthday tomorrow," Polly replied.

"Never say tomorrow's a bad day, my child," Grandma scolded her.

"I said, it's her BIRTHDAY tomorrow, Grandma," Polly shouted so loudly that grandma's cap trembled just a bit. "And, we're going to give her a surprise!"

"You don't say!" said Grandma as Polly skipped around and gave her a hug. "What's wrong with her eyes?"

"A birthday SURPRISE!" Polly stood on tiptoe and shouted right into Grandma's ear. "We want to bake her a cake!" Polly said. "Won't you please tell me how?"

"A cake for her birthday! That will be fine," Grandma said, righting her cap. "I have a grand cake recipe right here."

Grandma waddled over to the wooden table. She turned an old tin teapot upside down and a jumble of yellowed papers tumbled out. Grandma searched through the pile for her best cake recipe.

"Now first you start with the eggs—" said Grandma.

"Oh, we don't have eggs, Grandma," Polly interrupted. "We've only brown flour."

"Well, brown flour will do, and it will look good with the raisins—" Grandma said.

"Oh, we don't have raisins," Polly said, beginning to worry.

"No raisins! What were you going to put in the cake?" Grandma asked, looking at Polly over her glasses.

"Cinnamon. We've got plenty of that," Polly said. "We have to bake a cake for Mamsie. We just have to. It's her birthday," Polly added.

"You can use this recipe and make do with what you have at home," Grandma said, handing the crumbly yellow slip of paper to Polly.

"Thank you, Grandma!" Polly said, slipping the bit of paper into her pocket. "I must be getting back," she added, giving Grandma a quick kiss on her cheek.

Polly flew home and burst into the kitchen,

eyes dancing, ready to begin baking, when she saw a terrible sight.

It was Phronsie. She was huddled in the corner of Mamsie's great big rocking chair, a little heap of sadness. She was crying bitterly. Joel hovered over her looking more worried than Polly had ever seen him.

"What's the matter?" gasped Polly. She rushed over to Phronsie and gathered the sad little girl in her arms.

"I was hammering and—" Joel began nervously. "Oh, Phronsie, please don't cry," Joel said, nearly crying himself.

Just then, Davie burst in with a bottle of castor oil.

"Joel, tell me what happened," Polly said, "Or Davie, you tell me—right now—or else—"

"No, I'll tell," Joel said, "Really, I will."

Polly waited as Phronsie buried her head in Polly's shoulder and sobbed her heart out.

Joel took a deep breath and said all in a rush, "I was hammering, and the old hammer was shaking, and Phronsie stuck her foot in the way . . . and, oh, Polly, I didn't mean to do it—" Joel ended with a wail of his own.

Quick as a flash, Polly tore off Phronsie's little old shoe and well-worn sock, and tenderly took hold of Phronsie's fat, little foot. Joel and Davie watched in fear as Polly checked the chubby, white toes, working them back and forth, and up and down.

"Nothing's broken," Polly said at last with a grateful sigh.

"It hurts, Polly. Right there," Phronsie said through a rain of tears. She wiggled her big toe. Polly saw the small, black spot that was growing under the nail.

Just then, Polly heard a small and strange noise. She looked up and saw Joel, trying his hardest not to cry. Before she could say a word,

Joel flung himself into Polly's lap in a flood of tears.

"There, there, Joel, dear," Polly said, gathering him into her arms beside Phronsie. I know you didn't mean to do it." Polly dropped a kiss on his stubby brown head.

When Phronsie saw Joel crying, she immediately stopped. "Don't cry, Joel. Does your toe ache, too?" she asked, patting his head.

This made Joel cry even harder. To think that he'd hurt the baby, everyone's pet, was enough to make his heart break.

"Look here," Davie said, holding up the bottle of castor oil. "If we give Phronsie a spoonful of this, she'll feel all better," Davie added.

Phronsie took one look at the medicine bottle and began to cry all over again.

Polly didn't know what to do. Then the kitchen door opened, and in walked Grandma Bascom.

"I found it," Grandma said, waving another crumbly piece of paper in the air.

Then she saw the tragic scene in the little old kitchen.

"Mercy me. What is going on?" Grandma asked.

Little Davie poured out the whole story.

"What's he saying, Polly?" Grandma asked. "I can't understand a word of it."

"Try again, Davie," Polly told him.

So this time, Davie stood on tiptoe and shouted the details directly into Grandma's ear.

"We need wormwood!" Grandma cried after she inspected Phronsie's toe, which was quickly turning black and blue. "I've got some at home, hanging right by the fireplace."

"I'll get it. Please let me," Joel said, jumping up from the chair so suddenly that Grandma nearly dropped her glasses in surprise.

Joel flew out the door and returned with great speed, a bunch of herbs dangling in his hand.

"You'll be just fine," Grandma said as she wrapped a wet rag and the wormwood around Phronsie's toe.

Grandma reached into her pocket. She pulled out a little bundle.

"And these are for you, Polly," Grandma said. "I don't want them, and they'll make your cake go better."

Polly opened the bundle. It was filled with raisins!

"Oh, Grandma!" Polly exclaimed.

"They're awfully hard," Joel said, as he and Davie investigated the bundle.

Luckily, Grandma didn't hear Joel. Instead, she put on her shawl and moved toward the door.

"Mercy me, I almost forgot," she said. She held up a crumbly piece of yellow paper and handed it to Polly. "I found my best cake recipe after all!"

CHAPTER 2

Mamsie's Birthday Surprise

Polly bundled Phronsie's foot into one of Mamsie's old slippers.

Phronsie looked sadly at her tiny little shoe. "Will I ever be able to wear my new shoes again?" she asked.

"You'll be good as new in a week," Polly told her, handing Phronsie her favorite doll.

Phronsie hugged the old, worn doll close and smiled a bright little smile. She knew everything would be all right, because Polly had told her so.

"Now, we must begin," Polly said cheerfully. She put on her apron and bustled about the kitchen as Phronsie and her doll watched. Polly stepped over Joel and Davie, who wrestled on the kitchen floor, arguing over who would be more help.

"Boys, go and get me some cinnamon from the basement cupboard," Polly asked, even though she didn't need any more cinnamon for the cake. Davie and Joel went down to the basement.

Polly carefully measured the brown flour, water, butter, and cinnamon. She mixed it together with Grandma's raisins. She poured the batter into the cake tin, put it in the cranky, black stove and happily banged the door shut.

Polly took Phronsie into her arms and sat back to wait until the cake was done. That's when Polly heard a THUMP from the basement.

"Joel, Davie," Polly called. "Come up here this instant!"

Joel and Davie trooped up the stairs and into the kitchen. Their faces were dusty with cinnamon.

"What happened?" Polly asked.

Phronsie's eyes grew round and large.

"We were wrestling—" Davie began.

"The sack just fell over on us. Honest it did, Polly," Joel interrupted.

"Goodness. Let's get you cleaned up before Mamsie comes home," Polly said.

She jumped up and cleaned off their faces with a wet dishrag.

Phronsie saw it first. A wispy curl of black smoke rose above the cranky, old stove.

"Mamsie's cake!" Phronsie cried.

Polly raced over to the stove, yanked out the cake, and set it on the table.

Their beautiful cake was ruined. It was black on the top and the center had fallen in.

Polly turned around and shouted at the stove.

"I hope you're happy. You've spoiled our Mamsie's birthday, you mean, old thing!"

Without warning, Polly sank down to the middle of the floor and began to cry as hard as she could.

Phronsie, Davie, and Joel didn't know what to do.

"Well, well, what's happening here?" asked a kindly and cheery voice. Everyone turned around.

"Mrs. Beebe!" cried Davie. "Look, Polly. It's Mrs. Beebe."

Mr. and Mrs. Beebe owned the shoe shop in town. They had gone out for a ride to pick some flowers and buy some candies. On their way back to town, they heard the fuss in the Little Brown House and stopped to see if they could help.

Polly hopped to her feet, ashamed. She wiped away her tears. The children explained to Mrs.

Beebe about Mamsie's birthday the next day and why Polly was crying.

"My goodness, you poor things," Mrs. Beebe said over and over as she heard the sad story. "Here, my dear. Here are some flowers for you," Mrs. Beebe said, handing a bunch to Polly.

"Thank you, Mrs. Beebe," Polly said, smiling through her tears.

Polly looked sadly at the black top and deep hole in the center of the cake. Then she looked at the flowers in her hand.

"I know!" Polly exclaimed.

Polly placed the bunch of flowers in the hollow center of the cake. The flowers covered up the hole and the black top!

"It's beautiful," Phronsie said.

"It's perfect!" Mrs. Beebe agreed.

"Thank you, Mrs. Beebe," Polly said again, this time with a wide smile.

"We must get back to the shoe shop," Mrs.

Beebe said, pleased that all was well. "Oh, one more thing," she said, reaching into her pocket. "Here's a peppermint candy for each of you."

After Mrs. Beebe was gone, the Little Brown House was quiet once again.

"I wish the world were made of peppermint candy," Joel said as the last bit of peppermint melted on his tongue.

"I'm going to hide the cake away till tomorrow morning, so Mamsie can't find it," Polly said. She climbed on a chair and gently placed the cake on the top shelf of the highest cupboard.

"Now, during dinner, make sure that none of you look up at the cupboard and give away the surprise," Polly told them.

"Can't I open it a little crack and take one smell when Mamsie isn't looking?" Joel asked.

"No!" Polly said firmly. "Not one peek! Or she will guess the surprise."

But that evening Mrs. Pepper was too busy

listening to Phronsie and the story of her toe. She wouldn't have guessed if there were a hundred cakes in the cupboard.

After dinner, Ben took Phronsie off into a corner so she could tell him all about the events of the day.

"Don't you think it was mean of the stove to make Polly cry?" Phronsie asked.

"Yes I do," Ben said grimly. It hurt him to know that Polly had been sad.

"What are you staring at, Joel?" Polly asked as she cleaned up the dishes.

Joel was staring at the wall, his back to the cupboard.

"You told me not to look at the cupboard!" Joel said in a loud whisper.

"Oh dear, that will just make Mamsie suspect something," Polly said in a low voice.

"What's that about the cupboard?" Mamsie asked.

"We can't tell," said Phronsie, shaking her head at her mother, "because there's a ca—"

"Ben!" Polly said, hushing Phronsie with a hug. "Tell us a bedtime story!"

"Oh, yes!" the little Peppers cried.

As Ben told his story, one by one the little Peppers dropped off to sleep.

The next morning was Mamsie's birthday. The first thing Polly did was run to the cupboard, followed by everyone else, to see if the cake was safe. Polly placed it proudly on the kitchen table.

"It looks better than it did yesterday," Polly said. "Isn't it pretty with the flowers, Ben?"

"Looks good enough to eat, that's for sure," Ben said, smacking his lips.

"Everything's ready!" Polly said. "Let's call Mamsie."

Oh, how surprised their mother was when she saw the birthday cake. She was delighted and admired the cake on every side.

"I don't know how you could have made such a beautiful cake in that old stove," Mamsie said. Then she cut it and gave a piece to every child, with a little flower on top of each slice. The cake turned out to taste even better than it looked.

"Why can't I have a birthday?" asked Joel, licking the last crumb from his lip.

"You've had eight," Ben told him.

"Not a cake-birthday," Joel said. "I never had a cake-birthday, did I, Polly?"

"Someday you will," Polly assured him.

And, Joel knew that someday he would, because Polly had said so.

CHAPTER 3

Trouble and More Trouble!

A few weeks after Mamsie's birthday, Joel gazed unhappily at his bowl of oatmeal. "I wish we could have something else to eat," said Joel. "I'm tired of the same old breakfast."

"Well, hand it over then," said Ben, who was always hungry.

"Be grateful for what we've got, Joel," Mamsie gently scolded him as she kissed the top of his head. "Polly, remember to visit the parson today. He's a little bit sick." Then Mamsie went into the next room to begin work on her sewing for the day.

"Oh, dear," said Phronsie, pushing her bowl away. "I'm sick, too."

"You are?" Polly asked with alarm.

"I'm sick of oatmeal," Phronsie pouted. "Polly, will we ever have anything else to eat?"

"Someday we will," Polly said. "Someday we'll have lots and lots of good things and treats."

"Like what?" Phronsie asked.

The Little Peppers didn't have money for sweets or fancy foods. They only had enough to pay for oatmeal, flour, and potatoes.

Polly thought a moment.

"Someday we'll have ice cream and little cakes with sugar frosting," Polly said as she filled a tub of soapy water and cleared the breakfast dishes.

"With pink on top?" Phronsie asked, getting down from her seat to help Polly wash up.

"More pink icing than even you can eat, Phronsie Pepper," Polly laughed.

"I'd like plum puddings," Joel said. "Like the one Mamsie made us for Thanksgiving that one time. Seventy-five of them," he added, patting his stomach.

"I'd have roast beef and potatoes and pie!" Ben said, putting on his coat. "Come on, Joel. We'll be late to chop wood at Deacon Blodgett's."

Joel slowly got up and went with Ben.

"What would you choose, Davie?" Polly asked.

Davie had been quietly eating his oatmeal. He thought for a moment, and then put down his spoon.

"I think the most beautiful breakfast would be toasted white bread and candy!" Davie said.

"Oh, I think so, too!" Phronsie said excitedly, accidentally spilling Polly's washtub filled with soapy water.

"Phronsie!" Polly cried. "You're wetter than a hen in the rain!"

"Oh, help, it's running down my back!" Phronsie cried.

Polly took a dry towel from a nearby laundry basket and wrapped Phronsie up tightly. She pulled off Phronsie's dripping stockings, shoes and dress, which were forming little puddles of dishwater at her feet. Then she helped Phronsie into a clean, dry dress and settled her into her bedroom.

Mamsie came back into the kitchen just as Polly finished cleaning everything up.

"I think I'll take Phronsie with me to visit the Hendersons," said Polly.

She looked into the bedroom and saw Phronsie fast asleep in a heap on the floor, her face bright red.

"No, I won't after all," said Polly, as she pulled on her coat.

"Ask if Parson Henderson still has a chill, if

he has a fever, and how he slept last night. We wouldn't want anything to happen to the minister," Mamsie said in a worried voice. Then she added a whole list of new questions to be sure to ask the Hendersons.

"Oh, I'll never remember all that," Polly said in dismay.

"Yes you will," Mamsie said with a smile.

Polly knocked on Parson Henderson's old-fashioned green door with the heavy brass knocker. It was the fanciest house in Badgertown, and Polly was always a little bit nervous when she went there.

When the door opened, Polly's heart sank. Instead of gentle Mrs. Henderson, the parson's wife, there stood Miss Jerusha, the parson's very mean sister.

Miss Jerusha was a big woman with sharp black eyes and tiny glasses, which she wore on the tip of her nose. When she looked down her nose

and over her glasses at Polly, all of Mamsie's questions flew out of Polly's head.

"Well, what do you want?" Miss Jerusha asked sternly.

"I came to see—I mean my mother sent me," stammered poor Polly.

"And who is your mother and just where do you live?" Miss Jerusha asked, sounding very much like a police officer.

"I live on Promise Lane," said Polly. "My mother is Mrs. Pepper."

"Mrs. who?" Miss Jerusha asked.

By this time, Polly was so scared she nearly turned and ran away.

"Why it's Polly Pepper," a gentle voice said.

Mrs. Henderson came to the door and led Polly through the wide hallway into a big old-fashioned sitting room.

Miss Jerusha followed them. She sat down by the window and started to knit. Just as Polly was about to ask about Parson Henderson, the door to the sitting room opened and he walked in.

"Oh," said Polly, flustered all over again.

"What is it, my dear?" the kindly minister asked.

"I do hope you're not going to get a fever, be sick, and die!" she blurted out.

"Well I never!" Miss Jerusha exclaimed.

"I hope not as well, my dear," the minister smiled.

"Come outside and see our new brood of chicks, Polly," Mrs. Henderson said, rescuing her from Miss Jerusha.

While petting and holding the fuzzy little chicks, Polly was able to ask all the questions her mother had told her to say. Happy to know that everything at the Henderson's was well, Polly put the little puffballs back into their coop.

"I must be going, now," Polly said. "Mamsie will be needing me."

"Wait one minute," Mrs. Henderson said. She went into the kitchen and returned a moment later with a bowl full of fresh butter.

"My sister sent us some of her lovely butter, and we would like to share it with you," she said kindly.

"Oh, thank you, Mrs. Henderson. The little ones love butter," Polly exclaimed.

Polly hummed all the way home. She knew how happy Phronsie would be when she gave her a piece of bread with lots of butter.

"Phronsie!" Polly called as she came through the door.

"Hush, Polly!" said Mrs. Pepper from the great rocking chair in the middle of the floor. She was holding Phronsie in her arms.

"There's something wrong with Phronsie. She's covered with spots and burning up with fever. Go for Doctor Fisher, Polly. Run as fast as you can!" she said.

Polly put down the butter bowl and ran for the doctor. Polly knew in her heart that something bad was happening, for the Peppers had never sent for the doctor before.

"It's measles," Doctor Fisher declared after examining the poor little girl. "No cause for alarm. Have any of the others ever had it?" he asked Mrs. Pepper.

"No," Mrs. Pepper replied with a worried shake of her head.

Doctor Fisher mixed up some black-looking stuff in a bottle and gave a spoonful of it to Phronsie. Poor little Phronsie was so sick, she didn't even protest—not a bit!

"Polly," whispered Mrs. Pepper. "Run and get my purse."

Polly returned with the worn little purse where Mrs. Pepper's kept her hard-earned dollars. Slowly, Mrs. Pepper counted out the money she owed the doctor.

"No charge, Mrs. Pepper," Doctor Fisher said. "Call me whenever you need me," he added.

With that, he was gone, even before Mrs. Pepper could thank him for his kindness.

"What is measles?" Phronsie asked in a sleepy voice.

"Just something children get," Mrs. Pepper said with a sigh. "Although I was hoping it would pass all of you by."

"Well, I won't get it," Polly said. "Neither will any of the rest of us!"

While Mrs. Pepper put Phronsie to bed, Polly worked in the kitchen, getting lunch ready for Ben and Joel and Davie when they returned.

Just then, Joel and Davie tumbled into the kitchen, hungry as wolves.

"Where's Ben?" Polly asked, setting down a plate of buttered bread.

"He's just coming down the lane," Joel said between mouthfuls.

"He says he feels funny," piped up Davie.

"Something is wrong with Ben," Joel said.

Polly dropped the cup she held. It broke into a dozen pieces. *Something is wrong with Ben!*

Polly flew out the door and met Ben coming down the lane. His face looked just like Phronsie's!

"Oh, Ben," Polly cried. "You've got the measles!" She flung her arms around him.

"No, I don't, Polly," Ben assured her. "My head aches a bit, and my eyes feel funny. But I'll be fine after lunch," Ben said.

Mrs. Pepper took one look at Ben's red face and sighed. She gave him a spoonful of Phronsie's medicine and packed him off to bed.

Without Ben's wages, Mrs. Pepper would have to take in three times more sewing than she usually did. That meant Polly would have to help with the sewing, nurse the sick ones, and take care of the house.

For almost a week, Polly and Mrs. Pepper worked side by side and barely got a wink of sleep.

෴

One morning, Polly tried to get the sick ones to eat their breakfast. Neither Ben nor Phronsie could bear the sight of the usual oatmeal.

"Make them some toast and tea, Polly, dear," Mrs. Pepper said.

Mrs. Pepper was worn and worried. She'd been up all night, back and forth from Ben's bed to restless little Phronsie, who refused to sleep in her own bed and kept getting up to be with Polly.

Polly had tried to sit up the night with Phronsie. But somewhere in the middle of the night, she had fallen asleep, leaving her mother to care for both Phronsie and Ben. When Polly woke in the morning, she felt she had let her mother down. She vowed to work extra hard to take care of Ben and Phronsie during the day.

"Here you go," Polly said cheerfully as she brought Ben his toast and butter. Poor Ben pretended to eat, for Polly's sake, but he barely touched anything at all.

Next Polly went in to see Phronsie.

"My face itches," Phronsie wailed. She rubbed her face with both fat little hands. "I want Mamsie," she cried.

"Mamsie is sewing and can't come in," Polly said, offering Phronsie some toast.

Phronsie took a bite, but the bread was hard and dry. She cried harder than before.

"Now, Phronsie, I saw the cutest little chick yesterday. And it snapped up a bug from the mother hen in just one bite," Polly said as she heaped a pat of butter on a tiny piece of toast.

"It did?" Phronsie asked. "How?"

"Let me show you," Polly said. "Let's pretend

you're a little chick and I'm the mother hen. Open your mouth, just like this—"

Polly leaned her head back and opened her mouth. Phronsie did, too. Polly placed a bit of buttered toast on Phronsie's tongue. In spite of herself, Phronsie chewed the toast.

"Just like that!" Polly said, delighted.

Phronsie eyed the next piece of buttered toast and asked, "Did the little chick have two bugs?"

"Yes it did!" Polly said and popped another piece of buttered toast right into Phronsie's mouth. Soon every piece was gone.

That night, Polly offered to sit up with Ben to give him his medicine.

"No, Polly," Mrs. Pepper said. "You'll be worn out in the morning."

"Let me," said Davie. "I can do it."

"Davie is too little. He'll fall asleep," Polly whispered to her mother.

Then Ben came up with a plan.

"I'll tie a string to Davie's arm," Ben suggested. "When it's time for my medicine, I'll just wake him up,"

In spite of Ben's plan, Polly didn't get much sleep. Phronsie cried and called for water all night long. By morning, no one had gotten much sleep.

After breakfast, Mrs. Pepper handed Joel a coat for Mr. Peters, one of Mamsie's best customers. She had mended it during the night.

"Take this coat to Mr. Peters and be sure to wait for him to give you the money he owes us," Mrs. Pepper said.

"It's not nice up at the Peters's house," Joel grumbled as he took the coat and left.

"Let me help you with the sewing, Mamsie," Polly offered, taking some of the mending from her mother's lap.

Mr. Atkins, who owned the clothing store, had given Mrs. Pepper a week's worth of mending to do.

"You've done so much already," Mamsie sighed. "It can wait."

"No it can't," Polly said briskly. "We need the money. You know we do. Mr. Atkins won't give you next week's work if we don't finish this up today."

"I suppose you're right," Mrs. Pepper said, allowing Polly to take the sewing from her.

Davie tried his best to help out, too. He blundered through Ben's outdoor chores, chopping wood and stacking logs. But it took him twice as long to do the things that Ben did easily.

Meanwhile, Polly sewed all morning long to help her mother.

"Polly, dear, rest a bit," Mrs. Pepper said.

"I'm going to sew every day with you,

Mamsie," she promised. "That way Mr. Atkins will give us even more mending to do."

"I don't believe anybody's got such wonderful children as I do," Mrs. Pepper said, and gave Polly a kiss on the top of her head.

Hours later, Joel straggled into the Little Brown House, hungry as a bear.

"Where have you been all this time?" Mrs. Pepper asked.

"I've been at the Peters's house," Joel said, placing the money on the table.

"This whole time?" Mrs. Pepper said with surprise.

"Well, I gave him the coat, and then they all went about their business and didn't give me the money," Joel said, wolfing down the bread that Polly set before him.

"So what did you do?" Mrs. Pepper asked.

"I waited and waited. Then I told them that

we needed the money because Ben and Phronsie had the squeazles," Joel said, munching on the last of the bread.

"The measles," Polly corrected him.

"Then they laughed and gave me the money," Joel said. "I'm never going back!" he said, flinging himself onto the floor to take a nap.

All afternoon, Polly sewed and sewed. But it got harder for Polly to thread the needle. She rubbed her eyes, but that didn't help at all.

"Oh dear," Polly thought. "My eyes feel like there's sand in them."

Polly didn't want to let her mother down, so she kept on sewing until she was done.

"There now," Polly said, jumping up from her seat. "I'll do twice as much tomorrow!" Polly promised her mother.

That night, tired Polly tucked herself into her old four-poster bed and hoped she'd feel better in the morning.

But when morning came, Polly could hardly move. She dragged herself to look in the old cracked mirror beside her bed. Polly lost all hope when she gazed at her red reflection. The measles! She had it, too.

"I don't care if I do," Polly declared. "I can't be sick. I won't be sick. What will Mamsie do?"

Feeling awful, Polly got dressed and stumbled into the kitchen. She tried to set the table, but she couldn't see the dishes or the table very well at all.

"Polly!" Joel called, coming into the kitchen.

Polly jumped in surprise at Joel's voice. Then, without warning, she fell over in a heap.

"Mamsie! Something's wrong with Polly. She's fallen into the wood box!" Joel shouted.

CHAPTER 4

Hard Days for Polly

Doctor Fisher arrived in the middle of the morning to see what was the matter with Polly's eyes.

"Those eyes of yours have been used too much," the doctor said sharply. "What has Polly been doing?" he asked.

"Everything," Mrs. Pepper answered. "Polly does everything."

"Well, not anymore. Her eyes are very bad," the doctor announced.

"No! Don't make my Polly sick," Phronsie cried, throwing herself at the doctor's knees.

Doctor Fisher gently untangled Phronsie from his legs and placed her back into the bed.

"We're going to make Polly all well, little girl. She'll be able to see as good as new when we're done," Doctor Fisher assured her.

"Really?" Phronsie asked tearfully.

"We'll try our hardest," Doctor Fisher said. "But you have to promise me you won't cry. If you cry, then Polly will cry—and that will be very bad for Polly's eyes. Very bad indeed!" he repeated.

"I won't cry," Phronsie promised. "Not one bit!" She wiped off the last tear with her hand.

Doctor Fisher put some cooling lotion on Polly's eyes.

"Now you rest up, young lady, and your eyes will be fine," Doctor Fisher said before leaving the little brown house.

"My eyes don't feel a single bit better," Polly complained to Mrs. Pepper. "And, there's so much work to do—"

"You have to give it time, Polly," Mrs. Pepper said, taking up her sewing again. "Your poor eyes need rest. And that's that."

Just then the kitchen door slammed, and moments later, Grandma Bascom stood at the bedroom doorway.

"Mercy me. What's happening here?"

Grandma said, surprised to see Polly in bed in the middle of the day.

"Measles. Polly's got them," Mrs. Pepper said. "Ben and Phronsie, too," she added.

"Freezing? Polly's freezing?" Grandma squawked.

With a sigh, Mrs. Pepper stood up and shouted the whole, sad story into Grandma Bascom's ear.

"Well, I've got a recipe at home that can set everybody right," Grandma said, heading for the door.

"Doc Fisher just left," Mrs. Pepper explained. "He put some lotion on Polly's eyes and said they must not be touched."

"Well, then, maybe these treats will help," Grandma said. She reached into her apron pocket and pulled out a small cloth sack.

"What's that?" asked Joel. He eyed the little sack. Joel was always curious whenever anyone mentioned treats.

"Peppermints!" Joel cried when Grandma opened the bag.

"You share those with the sick ones," Grandma gently scolded him.

Joel handed out the peppermints to all the children, giving extra to Phronsie and Ben.

"I don't want any," Polly told him, pushing the peppermints away.

"Oh, Polly, you have to try one," Joel said, munching happily.

Polly was too sad to answer.

"I'll leave three on your pillow, Polly," Joel said. "You just take them whenever you want."

Then Joel and Davie went outside to share the rest of the peppermints and stack the wood in the woodpile.

Polly leaned back against the pillow. Who was going to help Mamsie now? How was all the work around the Little Brown House going to get done? Two big, fat tears rolled down her face.

Polly knew she wasn't supposed to cry, but she just couldn't help it.

Later that day, a carriage stopped right in front of the Peppers' little brown gate.

"It's the Hendersons!" exclaimed Mrs. Pepper.

Moments later, Mrs. Henderson was sitting beside Polly in the darkened bedroom.

"Poor little thing," Mrs. Henderson said, stroking Polly's hair.

"Oh, I don't care about my eyes. Only about helping Mamsie," Polly cried.

"Now, don't you worry about that," Mrs. Henderson assured her. "You just worry about getting better, so you can see the little chicks you visited the other day. You wouldn't believe how big and fat they are!"

"Oh, do tell me about them," Polly said, forgetting for a moment about the dreadful itching in her eyes.

By the time the Hendersons left, somehow a

basket of eggs, a sack of flour, a bowl of butter, and several loaves of bread had found their way out of their carriage and into the Pepper's little kitchen.

Weeks went by, and Polly's eyes did not get better. One day, after Doctor Fisher had checked Polly's eyes and was about to leave, Mrs. Pepper stopped him.

"Doctor Fisher, you must tell me the truth. Will our little Polly be blind from now on?" Mrs. Pepper asked. Her face was lined with worry.

"She just needs more time," Doctor Fisher said. "You have to try to keep her spirits up. That's the most important thing of all. Then she'll be good as new."

"I'm all better," Phronsie said.

"Yes, you are," Doctor Fisher said, patting Phronsie's golden head. "Tell me something," he whispered, kneeling beside Phronsie. "What does Polly want most of all in the world?" he asked her.

"I know," Phronsie said, nodding her head wisely. She leaned over and whispered in the doctor's ear, "Polly wants a stove!"

"She's already got one," he said, pointing to the old black stove in the corner of the kitchen.

"Oh, it's a nasty old thing. It won't burn right, and Ben has to stuff it up because it has a big, old hole. Sometimes, Polly cries when she thinks she's all alone, too. But I see her," Phronsie told him quietly.

"Well, then," the doctor said. "We shall have to do something about that."

After many weeks, things were almost back to normal in the Little Brown House. Ben was all better and working at Deacon Blodgett's. Mamsie had gone out to pick up more work from the Atkins's store. Even Phronsie was all better and tried her best to help. Only poor Polly still wore a bandage over her eyes and couldn't see a thing.

One day, Joel was left alone with Polly while everyone else was out. He was telling Polly how he wanted to be a minister just like Parson Henderson when there was a knock at the door.

"I'll get it," Joel said, opening the door.

"Well, well," said a stern voice from the doorway. "Who are you?"

Polly's heart sank as she recognized the voice. It was Miss Jerusha Henderson, the parson's unpleasant sister. It was her job to visit those in the village who were sick.

"Speak up, boy. How old are you?" Miss Jerusha asked Joel.

"I-I-I'm Joel. I-I-I'm nine years old," he stammered.

"Well, that makes you old enough to help your mother out with the chores, now doesn't it?" Miss Jerusha asked with a sniff.

"I do help Mother," Joel said. "I do lots and lots of things."

"And you, girl," said Miss Jerusha, turning towards Polly. "Don't you greet your guests when they come to visit you? What have you been doing with yourself all these days?"

"I'm sorry, I can't see to do anything," Polly said unhappily.

"You could knit," Miss Jerusha said. "When I was a little girl your age, I had sore eyes, and I was able to knit."

"Were you ever little?" Joel asked. He couldn't believe a woman as big and mean as Miss Jerusha had ever been Polly's age.

"Little boys shouldn't speak unless they're spoken to," Miss Jerusha scolded Joel. "Now, tell me, girl. Have you ever knit a stocking?"

"No," Polly said, shaking her head.

"Really! Imagine that. A big girl like you has never knit a stocking! To think your mother should have raised you this way—" Miss Jerusha started to say.

"Our mother brought us up just right. And don't you say she didn't," Joel shouted, his eyes blazing and his face red.

"Well, you certainly are a rude little boy," Miss Jerusha said as she stood up to leave. "Now when I come back again, Polly, I expect to see what sort of knitting you have done."

"You're never coming here again!" said Joel angrily. "Not ever!"

"Mercy me!" Miss Jerusha said. "What will your mother have to say about this!"

"Joel, be quiet!" Polly begged him.

Polly was so upset she pulled off her eye bandages.

"I don't know what's got into him. Joel is always so good," Polly said.

"It's clear you've all been spoiled from the day you were born. To think of how hard your mother works and neither of you do a single thing to help her," Miss Jerusha scolded.

"Oh, please don't say that," Polly cried, and she burst into a flood of tears.

"No! Don't make Polly cry. You'll kill her!" Joel shouted at Miss Jerusha. He ran to Polly and put both arms around her neck to hug her. "Please, Polly, don't cry!" Joel pleaded.

"I won't waste another minute on such an ungrateful family," Miss Jerusha said with a sniff as she disappeared out the door.

Even after Miss Jerusha was long gone, Polly continued to sob as though her heart would break.

"Please, Polly. Please stop crying," Joel begged, almost in tears himself. "I'll go get Ben," he added.

That stopped Polly's crying at once.

"No, you must not trouble Ben," Polly said, wiping the tears from her eyes. "Oh, my eyes ache so badly," Polly told him.

She twisted and turned in pain.

"Let's put some water on them, Polly," Joel said. "I'll get you some," He couldn't bear to see his sister in pain.

"No, the doctor won't allow it," Polly said. "I wish Mamsie was back from the Atkins's store."

Joel peeped out the window. "Here she is, now, Polly, coming up the lane!"

CHAPTER 5

Measles, Measles Everywhere!

⤳

Mrs. Pepper stepped brightly into the Little Brown House, sure that her worries were soon to end.

"Polly? Joel?" she called as she walked into the bedroom. She saw Polly holding her eyes as if they might fly out of her head, while Joel stood helplessly beside her.

"My goodness! What in the world happened here?" she asked.

"That big, old, mean woman made our Polly

cry her eyes out," Joel explained. "And now her eyes feel worse—"

"Crying? Polly's been crying?" Mrs. Pepper repeated.

"Oh, Mamsie. I couldn't help it. Miss Jerusha said—" Polly stopped. A rain of tears began again.

"Hush now, my girl," Mrs. Pepper said. She gathered up Polly into her arms as though she were little Phronsie.

"I know I shouldn't have minded what she said, but—" Polly started to say—

"What did she say?" Mrs. Pepper asked.

Between them, Polly and Joel explained the whole thing. Although she didn't say it aloud, Mrs. Pepper vowed to herself that Miss Jerusha Henderson would never visit the Little Brown House again.

"There, there, Polly dear. You are truly the best daughter a mother could have. Don't think about a word that Miss Henderson said," Mrs.

Pepper said soothingly. "You must stop crying and save your eyes."

But the damage was already done. Over the next few days, Polly's eyes hurt more than ever. There was nothing to be done to soothe them.

When Doctor Fisher came to examine Polly and heard what had happened, his expression grew very serious. Polly had been almost well the last time he'd been to visit. But now—

Just then, Phronsie ran in, crying "Polly! Mamsie says Joel's sick. Come quick!"

Without a second thought, Polly jumped right up and tore off the eye bandages. "I will help Mother. I will!" Polly declared, heading for Joel's bedroom.

Doctor Fisher gently and firmly sat Polly back in her chair.

"Polly Pepper, you must not take off those bandages again," Doctor Fisher explained. "If you do, you will surely go blind and your mother will have to care for you all her life! Now, I'll see to Joel, and you do your part by staying still."

Joel was very sick. For days, his life was at risk. No one in the Little Brown House spoke above a whisper. No one ever said aloud how worried he or she was about him. Things were so bad at the Little Brown House that their neighbor Mrs. Beebe came to stay and help.

One afternoon, when Polly couldn't stand it a minute longer, she flung herself down on the bed and buried her face in the bed cover.

"Dear God. I'll give up my eyes. Make me blind if only you'll make Joel well," Polly whispered over and over.

Polly fell asleep for the first time since Joel had become sick. Mrs. Beebe came in and found her.

"Polly, dear," Mrs. Beebe said, gently shaking Polly awake. "I've got something to tell you about Joel—"

Polly sat up, fearing the worst.

"He's going to get well. The danger is gone," Mrs. Beebe said.

"Really?" Polly cried. She jumped up and hugged Mrs. Beebe with all her strength.

"He'll be running and tumbling around in no time. Good as new," Mrs. Beebe said with a smile.

Sure enough, in a very few days, Mrs. Beebe's words came true.

CHAPTER 6

Polly's Surprise

⌒∽

Once Joel was all better, things got almost back to normal in the Little Brown House.

"Oh, I wish Doctor Fisher would hurry and get here so he can take off these bandages once and for all!" Polly said.

"He'll be here tomorrow, Polly," Mrs. Pepper reminded her.

"I can't wait either!" Davie blurted out. Then he clapped his hand over his mouth and buried his head in Mrs. Pepper's lap.

The other little Peppers could barely contain their excitement. They all knew a very important secret that was going to happen that day. Everyone except Polly knew, that is, because the secret was about her.

"I'm afraid I'll tell her," Davie whispered.

"No, you won't," Mrs. Pepper assured him. "But we must all do our best to keep Polly busy and out of the kitchen today."

"Play a game," Ben suggested.

"Play in the other room, and let me get busy in the kitchen," Mamsie added.

Ben led Polly and the other children into the living room. Then Ben sneaked back into the kitchen.

Polly, Phronsie, Davie, and Joel clapped and stamped and shouted. They could hardly hear the scraping and grating noises coming from the kitchen.

"Oh, look, I see the——" Phronsie sang out.

Davie swooped in and tickled her before she could spoil the surprise.

"What is that scraping noise?" Polly finally asked.

"I'll go see," Joel said and flew into the kitchen.

There, Joel saw his mother and Ben and two men at work on a big, black thing in the corner. The old stove was nowhere to be seen. In its place was a shiny new one, with lots of doors and burners.

"I bet Polly will be able to bake me a beautiful birthday cake in that someday," Joel said.

"You haven't told her, have you, Joel?" Mrs. Pepper asked.

"No, but Polly can hear all the noise. She wants to know what it is. What will I do?" he asked.

"Play tag. Sing a song. Do anything. We're almost done," Ben said.

Luckily, when Joel got back to the bedroom,

Polly was busy nursing Phronsie's newly hurt finger. Polly had forgotten all about the noise in the kitchen.

The next morning, it seemed as if the Little Brown House would turn inside out with joy.

Doctor Fisher untied the bandage around Polly's eyes. Her eyelids fluttered a bit in the darkened bedroom. They she opened her eyes wide. The first thing Polly saw was her mother's smiling face.

"Oh, Mamsie," Polly cried, jumping into her mother's arms. "My eyes are new! It's as if I just got them. Do they look different?" Polly asked, running to the cracked mirror to see for herself.

"They look like the same merry, brown eyes you always had," Ben said with a big grin.

"Well," Polly said, hugging each of her brothers and sisters in turn, "everybody looks different through them anyway!"

"Let's go into the kitchen, Polly," Joel said. "It's so much nicer out there."

The other children led Polly into the kitchen. She was ready to roll up her sleeves and start her work in the kitchen when she stopped and turned as pale as snow. She looked like she was going to tumble right over. Mrs. Pepper grabbed Polly to steady her.

"What is it?" Polly asked, pointing to the corner.

"It's a stove. Don't you know that, Polly?" Phronsie said.

Polly raced across the kitchen and flung her arms around the big, black, shiny stove. She was laughing and crying all at the same time.

All the children were so excited they began to speak at once. They joined hands and danced around like wild things. Mrs. Pepper laughed until she cried.

From the doorway, Doctor Fisher smiled at the happy scene. Then, he quietly left the Little Brown House for what he hoped would be the last time.

"We're never going to have any more burnt bread," Polly sang, all out of breath.

"And no big cracks to stuff with paper," Ben shouted.

"Hurray!" screamed Joel and Davie.

Phronsie gurgled and giggled through it all.

"Oh, I wish Doctor Fisher had seen it! Where did he go?" Polly asked, looking around.

"I think Doctor Fisher has seen it before," Mrs. Pepper said with a smile. "Wouldn't you like to know where the stove came from, Polly?" she asked.

Polly had been so overcome by surprise, she hadn't even thought to wonder.

"Did Doctor Fisher bring it?" Polly asked.

"Well, he didn't actually put it in the kitchen. But he had a great deal to do with picking it out and sending it over," Mrs. Pepper replied.

"Doctor Fisher bought us a stove! And, he saved my eyes." Polly said. "Oh, Mamsie. Doctor Fisher is the most wonderful doctor in the world. I'm going to bake him the most beautiful cake— right here in our brand, new stove!"

True to her word, Polly set to work at once. It made Mamsie's heart sing to see Polly happy and busy once more.

❧

A few weeks later, Polly was busy in the kitchen. Phronsie was playing in the garden. Suddenly, they both heard the sweet sound of music coming from down the lane.

"Oh, look, Phronsie. Come quick!" Polly called.

Through the window, Polly saw an organ grinder playing music with all his might. Beside him, on a long rope, was a lively, little monkey in a bright, red coat and a straw hat.

Phronsie and Polly hurried over to the organ grinder and his monkey. As they got close, the little monkey pulled off his hat, and with one long jump, he landed in front of Phronsie and bowed like a gentleman before her.

Phronsie wasn't a bit frightened. She held out her hand and gently said, "Poor little monkey. Come here."

The organ man pulled the monkey's rope, struck up another tune, and in a minute the monkey spun around and around, doing strange little dances to the music. He made Polly and Phronsie laugh and laugh.

When he was done, the organ grinder took off his cap and held it out, waiting for coins.

"Oh, I can't pay you," Polly said. She thought a moment. "But I can give you something to eat." Polly ran into the house and returned with brown bread and two potatoes.

"Is that all you've got?" the organ man asked angrily. He threw the bread to the ground, which the monkey gratefully snapped up. Then he turned and roughly pulled the monkey down the dusty road, away from the Little Brown House.

Polly went back to her work in the kitchen. Phronsie went back to the garden. At least, that's what Polly thought.

"Phronsie! It's lunchtime," Polly called as she walked through the garden to find Phronsie. Instead, all she found was Phronsie's baby doll on the ground. Phronsie was gone!

Polly and Ben searched everywhere. So did the rest of the family. In the course of an hour, the whole town knew that Phronsie had disappeared. All the good people of Badgertown were searching the dusty roads for her, but she was nowhere to be found.

"She must have followed the organ man and his monkey," Polly said tearfully.

"Or, the organ man just took her," Ben said grimly.

"What will we do?" Polly cried.

"I'll take Deacon Brown's horse and search the road to the next town," Ben decided. "He must have been headed that way."

In a flash, Ben raced down the road in Deacon Brown's horse and cart. He traveled ten miles, peering into every bush along the road. There wasn't a trace of Phronsie anywhere. The hot sun poured down on poor Ben's face. Deacon Brown's horse grew tired.

"Come on, boy," Ben cried out. "We can't go home without her."

Suddenly the horse stopped and Ben tumbled out of the cart. On the side of the road, was a boy who was slightly bigger than Ben, with a big, black dog by his side. The dog was protecting a pink bundle.

That pink bundle was Phronsie!

"Who are you?" the bigger boy asked Ben. The black dog's ears stood straight up at attention.

"I'm Ben Pepper," Ben replied. "And, that's my sister Phronsie!"

The bigger boy held out his hand. "I'm Jasper, and this is Prince."

"Why do you have my sister?" Ben asked.

"Prince and I saw that nasty organ grinder and his monkey walking down the road with Phronsie. She was crying, and when she saw Prince and me, she ran right up to us and said, 'I want Polly!'" Jasper told Ben. "The organ man grabbed her hand to pull her along, and then we went for him, Prince and I."

Jasper scratched Prince between the ears.

"Prince just kept after them until they both ran clear off down the road. They won't be back!" Jasper said with a laugh. "If you hadn't come along when you did, I was going to pick her up and take her home with me," Jasper said. "Then Father and I would have figured out what to do next."

Together Ben and Jasper put Phronsie into Deacon Brown's cart without waking her.

"Thank you, Jasper—and Prince," Ben said, shaking Jasper's hand once again, and patting

Prince on the head. "Come visit us at the Little Brown House sometime. I know Mother and Polly would love you to," Ben added.

"I will!" Jasper said, waving good-bye as Ben drove the horse and cart back home with his bundle safely tucked into the back.

CHAPTER 7

Jasper Comes to Visit

That afternoon, Jasper returned to the hotel
where he and his father were staying for the
summer.

"This hotel can't do anything right," Mr. King
grumbled. "There's no newspaper in the morning. The tea is always cold. The rooms are cold.
We'd be better off returning to the city," he
complained.

"Oh, but Father, I met Ben Pepper today. And
his sister, Phronsie, who is the sweetest, cutest

little thing you're ever likely to meet. They have a sister named Polly as well. I'd like to visit them over in the next town. May I, Father?" Jasper asked. Prince stood at Jasper's side, his ears up as if to ask Mr. King's permission as well.

"Peppers? I've never heard of a family with that name. What's all this about, Jasper?" Mr. King asked grumpily.

Jasper explained the whole rescue to Mr. King. In the meantime, Mr. King's newspaper finally arrived. His tea was hot, and the heater came on in the room. So, he agreed to stay at the hotel for a little bit longer. And, he gave Jasper permission to visit the Peppers.

The next day, Ben was in the yard chopping wood for Polly's new stove while Polly was busy cleaning in the kitchen.

"Hello!" said a familiar voice.

Ben looked up to see Jasper King and Prince standing in the lane.

"Jasper!" Ben said with a big grin.

In a flash, Polly was out the door. Without thinking, she flew to Prince and flung her arms around his neck.

"You must be Polly," Jasper said.

Embarrassed, Polly stood up and with a red face and held out her hand to Jasper.

"Forgive me. We're just all so grateful that you and Prince saved our little girl," Polly said, her voice choked with emotion.

Just then, Phronsie ran out the door right over to Prince. She wrapped her arms around his neck and buried her face in his smooth black fur.

Joel and Davie came into the front yard to see what all the commotion was about. Instantly, they made friends with Jasper and Prince. Ben showed Jasper around the Little Brown House. Joel and Davie happily played fetch with Prince. Polly and Phronsie told Jasper about the measles and the old black stove. Before long, it seemed as though Jasper and the Peppers had been friends forever.

Jasper sat happily in the kitchen and watched Polly make bread.

"I wish I knew how to bake," Jasper said.

"Mamsie and I will teach you when you come back," Polly said. "If you want us to," she added shyly.

"I'd like that," Jasper said. "It's no fun spending the summer in the hotel with only Father and Prince to talk to."

"Where's your mother?" Joel asked, wrestling on the floor with Prince and Davie.

There was an awkward silence.

Jasper lowered his eyes to the floor. "I don't have a mother," he replied in a soft voice.

No mother! Polly couldn't imagine how anybody would feel without a mother. Her heart ached for the boy who'd rescued their Phronsie.

"Then, I hope you'll come back every day," Polly told him.

At that moment, Mrs. Pepper walked in. Her gaze swept over the kitchen and rested on Jasper. She looked into his merry brown eyes, which twinkled just like Polly's. "You must be the boy who saved my little girl," she said.

"It was mostly Prince, Mrs. Pepper," Jasper murmured.

"You'll never know just how much you did," Mrs. Pepper said, giving Jasper a beautiful smile. "I hope you'll stay with us for dinner," she offered.

Jasper jumped up. "I'm afraid I can't. If I miss the coach back to the hotel, Father will never let me come back. Come, Prince," Jasper called.

"Oh, please stay," Phronsie begged. "Please?"

"I'll come again, if that's all right with you," Jasper asked Mrs. Pepper.

"You're always welcome here, Jasper King. Just make sure it's all right with your father," Mrs. Pepper added.

"I'll be back on Thursday!" Jasper called happily as he bounded out the door.

CHAPTER 8

The Gingerbread Boy

Thursday came and went, but Jasper didn't arrive.

The little Peppers were very disappointed. They had been looking forward with all their hearts to seeing Jasper and Prince again.

"It was probably his mean, old father," Polly said, wiping away a tear. "I know he would have come if he could have."

"Well, he promised to come, and he didn't," Joel said angrily. "I don't care if ever comes back."

"Joel, you should be ashamed of yourself. Jasper will come again. He will have a very good reason for why he didn't come today, too," Mrs. Pepper said.

The next day, when Ben was at the general store to buy more flour, Mr. Atkins called out to him. He held up an envelope.

"There is a letter here for your sister Polly," Mr. Atkins said.

"It can't be for Polly," Ben said. "She's never gotten any letters before. None of us have."

"Well, it says her name right here—Polly Pepper," Mr. Atkins said, pointing to the envelope.

Ben could hardly believe it. A letter for Polly! Ben raced home as fast as he could. He ran through the house calling for Polly, until he could place the envelope into her hands. Everyone gathered around to see whom it could be from.

Polly opened the letter and read it aloud,

Dear Polly,

I was so sorry I couldn't come on Thursday, but my father was sick and I couldn't leave him. I had a cold, too. If you're willing to have me, though, I'd like to come again.

Your friend,
Jasper King

⟡

"I want to make some lovely little cakes for Jasper," Polly said. "Can we, Mamsie? Please?"

"We don't have any white flour, Polly," Mamsie said, looking up from her sewing.

"I can make them with brown flour, and raisins. I know we have some," Polly said, heading for the cupboard.

"I was saving those for plum pudding," Mrs. Pepper said.

"No, don't give Jasper our raisins!" Joel yelled. "I want plum pudding. I do, I do. And Jasper doesn't deserve them," he added.

"Joel Pepper! You should never have plum pudding again for saying something like that about Jasper. He rescued Phronsie, and we owe him all our thanks. Don't you forget it," Mrs. Pepper scolded.

"Nevermind, Joel," Polly said, comforting him. "If you don't want me to use the raisins, I won't. It's just that Jasper's sick. Remember how you felt when you had the measles? You liked it when people sent you lovely things to eat, didn't you?"

Joel hung his head in shame.

"I'm sorry, Polly. I didn't mean it. Let's give Jasper all the raisins. Every last one of them!" Joel offered.

Joel and the others got busy helping Polly prepare the little cakes.

Mrs. Pepper smiled to herself to see her little brood so happy and busy.

"Now," said Phronsie, "I will bake a gingerbread boy for my poor, sick friend."

"You don't have to, Phronsie," Polly said. "One of the little cakes can be from you to Jasper."

Phronsie shook her yellow head. "Not Jasper."

"Do you mean Prince?" Polly asked, whipping up the batter for the cakes.

"No!" Phronsie said. "My poor, sick friend," she repeated.

"What do you mean?" Polly asked, dropping a lump of dough on the table.

"I want to make a gingerbread boy. That's what he'd like best!"

"Who?" Joel asked, pouncing on the lump of raisin-filled dough.

"Jasper's daddy!" Phronsie said.

"But, Phronsie," Polly started to say.

"A gingerbread boy!" Phronsie insisted, and she would not have it any other way.

⁓

After several hours, the cakes were done.

"They're beautiful little cakes, Polly," Joel said.

"My gingerbread boy is the most beautiful of all," Phronsie said, holding up a lumpy gingerbread figure with one raisin eye, two crooked legs, and stubby arms.

"Oh, what will Mr. King think of us," Polly whispered to Ben. "We can't let her send that."

"Better let me and Davie have him," Joel said, reaching for the lump of gingerbread.

"No!" shrieked Phronsie. "That's my sick friend's gingerbread boy. It is!"

"Nevermind," Polly said to comfort the little girl. "We'll send the gingerbread boy after all," she promised.

"How shall we send it?" Polly asked. "We don't have any nice baskets except for Mamsie's sewing basket. And, she needs that," Polly frowned.

"We can wrap the cakes in paper," Ben suggested. "I've got a nice piece upstairs."

They wrapped up the cakes and the gingerbread boy and set the package on the table.

"I wish we had some flowers to put on top of the paper," Polly said with a sigh.

"How about writing him a letter?" Mrs. Pepper suggested. "It's polite to reply to a letter with one of your own."

"But I've never written a letter before," Polly said, her cheeks turning pink and warm. "I can't!"

"There's a first time for everything, Polly dear," Mrs. Pepper said. "Never say you can't, because you don't know until you've tried."

"There now, I have something for you," Mrs. Pepper said. She went to her bedroom and took out a yellowed piece of fine writing paper from her top dresser drawer. She placed it on the kitchen table in front of Polly. Ben brought the ink bottle and the pen.

"What shall I say?" Polly asked with dismay.

"Tell him about the cakes and Phronsie's gingerbread boy. Let him know we'd like him to visit when he's well," Mrs. Pepper said, returning to her sewing.

Polly set to work over the paper, biting her lip as she wrote. At last she was done.

"Read it to us, Polly," Mrs. Pepper said.

Dear Jasper,

We knew you were sick because you didn't come. We liked your letter telling us so because we'd all felt so badly, and Phronsie cried herself to sleep.

*The "gingerbread boy" is for your father—please
excuse it. Phronsie insisted on making it for him
because he is sick. There isn't any more to write, and
besides I don't write very well, and Ben's too tired to
write any more.*

From all of us,

Ben and Polly signed the letter. The others
wanted to sign it too. Ben held Davie's hand and
helped him sign his name. Phronsie insisted that

Polly help her. Joel wanted to do it himself, and he dropped a great big blot of ink on the letter and nearly ruined it.

At long last, the letter was done and tied up with the package. Just then, Deacon Blodgett and his wife stopped by to say hello. They brought a lovely bunch of flowers for the family.

When Polly saw the flowers, she clapped her hands for joy. "Flowers just make everything happier. I wish I had flowers for every day of the year," she said. Then Polly tied the pretty flowers onto the package. It was lovely. Everyone agreed.

CHAPTER 9

A Surprise Guest

ᘒ

True to his word, as soon as Jasper recovered from his cold, he returned to visit the Peppers. They were delighted to see him.

Jasper told them all about how the package of little cakes made both him and his father feel better almost at once.

"I gave Prince the biggest one of all," Jasper added. "You must show me how to bake, Polly," he begged.

While Jasper finished telling about the package,

Polly prepared the kitchen for Jasper's baking lesson.

"What about my poor, sick friend?" Phronsie asked. "Did he like his gingerbread boy?"

"Very much indeed," Jasper said with a twinkle in his eye.

Phronsie trotted off to play in the corner with Prince.

Polly showed Jasper how to measure the flour and water and butter to make a piecrust. She taught him how to roll out the dough with a rolling pin.

"Did your father really like Phronsie's gingerbread man?" Polly asked.

"I've never seen him so happy," Jasper said with a smile. "In fact, he liked it so much, he propped it up on his writing desk so he could look at it all the time."

Polly sighed with relief, glad to know that Mr. King had not been offended.

"You know," Jasper said, putting the piecrust that Polly had helped him make into the oven, "You could cook a wonderful Thanksgiving dinner in this stove."

"We've never had a Thanksgiving. Nothing to make for it," Ben said lightly, as if he didn't really care.

"Never had Thanksgiving?" Jasper said with surprise. "What about Christmas dinner?"

"Nope. Never had a Christmas either," Davie said. "What are they like?" he asked.

Jasper sat quite still and didn't answer. He had never met anyone who hadn't had Thanksgiving or Christmas. He didn't understand.

"They hang up stockings and have a tree and a great big, lovely dinner," Polly explained patiently to Davie. "We will, too, someday, when our ship comes in. Isn't that right, Ben?" Polly said proudly.

"Absolutely right," Ben agreed.

At that moment, Jasper made a silent promise to himself. *"They will have a Christmas this year,"* he muttered.

Then Jasper told them stories of all his past Christmases. The Peppers listened with amazement. They were so amazed by Jasper's stories, they completely forgot about the baking. Suddenly, a horrible burning smell filled the kitchen.

"Oh, no!" Jasper cried, running to the stove. He pulled out a black, smoking mass.

"I've made a terrible mess of everything," Jasper said sadly, showing the ruined piecrust to Polly.

"That's okay," Polly said kindly. "Tell us more about Christmas," Polly said.

"There's always lots of music and dancing," Jasper began.

"Music!" cried Polly, clapping her hands. "Does anyone play the piano?" she asked.

"Polly's crazy about music, especially the piano," Joel said, looking at the burned piecrust to see if there was anything he could rescue to eat. "She's always pretending to play on the kitchen table," he added.

"Well, maybe someday you'll play on a real piano," Jasper said hopefully.

"That is a lovely dream," Polly said.

For the rest of the summer, Jasper spent every day he could at the Little Brown House. Mr. King, noticing how happy Jasper was, decided that perhaps their hotel wasn't such a bad place to spend the summer after all.

༄

At summer's end, a grand carriage drawn by a pair of handsome horses turned onto Promise Lane. It stopped right in front of the Little Brown House.

A tall, portly gentleman, leaning on a heavy gold-headed cane walked up from the little brown gate. Jasper and Prince followed behind him.

Polly opened the door.

"Is this little Miss Pepper?" Mr. King asked in a booming voice.

"I don't know, sir. I'm Polly," she stammered, blushing a deep rose-red.

"Is your mother in?" Mr. King asked, bending his head to peer through the front door.

"Mr. King, won't you come in?" Mrs. Pepper asked, coming up behind Polly.

Seated at the kitchen table, Mr. King looked around at all the smiling faces. "Where is the little girl who baked my gingerbread boy?" he asked.

Phronsie, who had been hiding in the corner, came up to the old gentleman, shaking her little yellow head. She climbed up and perched herself on his knee. "Poor, sick man. Was my little gingerbread boy good?"

"He was indeed!" Mr. King said.

Jasper and Prince and Mr. King spent the next few hours in the small, busy kitchen, happily chatting and laughing. The goodness and cheeriness of the Peppers warmed the old gentleman's heart.

"We came to tell you that we'll be leaving tomorrow," Mr. King said, as he rose to go. "Will you give me a kiss, my little girl?" he asked as he bent his handsome old head down to Phronsie's upturned face.

"Don't go," Phronsie said, giving him a peck on the cheek. "I do like you. I do!"

The rest of the little Peppers were very sad. Jasper was leaving! Losing Jasper and Prince felt almost as terrible as losing Ben, Joel, or Davie.

"I'll write," Jasper said, trying to cheer everyone up. "You must promise to write me back."

"We will," the little Peppers solemnly assured him, holding back their tears.

As Mr. King's carriage drove away, the Peppers went into their Little Brown House and shut the door.

CHAPTER 10

The First Real Christmas

That winter, letters flew back and forth between Jasper and the Peppers. Jasper wrote to Mrs. Pepper as well.

Remembering Jasper's wonderful stories about his many Christmases, Polly and Ben decided to make a real Christmas for the little Peppers. They told Mrs. Pepper their plan. To their great surprise, she agreed it was a fine idea.

"We must have a tree, just like Jasper's," Ben said.

"We'll decorate it with candles and things so it looks just as elegant as can be!" Polly cried.

"We'll have to make our plans after the little ones are asleep," Ben whispered. "Otherwise, they'll know, and it will spoil the surprise."

Polly and Ben worked as hard as they could to come up with presents for the little ones and decorations for their first Christmas tree.

Every night, after the younger children went to bed, Ben and Polly sat around the kitchen table with Mrs. Pepper. While she sewed by candlelight, they made ornaments out of colored paper. They sewed strings of popcorn and cranberries.

Then they made presents for the children's stockings. Polly made a paper doll for Phronsie from the leftover bits of colored paper. Ben carved windmills and whistles for the boys and a little basket with a handle for Phronsie. Mrs. Pepper sewed a pink dress and a little bonnet for Phronsie's baby doll. She knitted some mittens for Joel and Davie. Then she and Polly made taffy to put into the stockings, too.

"We will have the best Christmas of anyone," Polly said joyfully as she looked at the growing pile of presents laid out on the table.

"It's almost as much fun getting ready for Christmas as it is to have Christmas Day," Ben said as he carved away.

Mrs. Pepper smiled an odd little smile. She'd had a secret letter from Jasper about Christmas, but she had not said a word to Ben and Polly. Jasper's plans would be their Christmas surprise.

The weeks flew by, until it was only three days to Christmas.

"Where should we put the tree?" Polly wondered. "We can't put it in the kitchen—the little ones will see it."

"The storage room next to the house is the best place for it," Mrs. Pepper suggested.

Ben and Polly agreed.

The next day, Mrs. Pepper told Joel and Davie and Phronsie that it was time to hang their Christmas stockings.

Joel let out a whoop of delight. He and Davie turned the house upside down, looking for the biggest stockings they could find to hang over the fireplace. Phronsie carefully chose her brightest, reddest stocking to hang. "So Santa will know which one is mine," she said quietly.

"Will Santa know which one is mine?" Joel worried.

"Santa is very smart," Mrs. Pepper assured him.

On Christmas Eve, everyone was so excited and the little ones were so full of questions, Polly was sure no one would get a wink of sleep.

"Will Santa really come down the chimney?" Joel asked.

"Will he be all covered with soot?" asked Davie.

"Will he bring something for my doll?" Phronsie asked with concern.

"Yes, no, and yes!" Polly said, eager to get the little ones off to bed so she and Ben could fill their stockings before morning.

"I'm going to stay up all night so I can see Santa," Joel vowed.

"Me, too," Davie said.

But soon enough, Joel and Davie nodded off, and Ben carried them into bed. After giving her red stocking a good night kiss, Phronsie crept into bed as well. As Polly tucked Phronsie in for the night, the little girl's eyes were happy and bright.

"I wish I had something to give Santa," she whispered.

Polly's heart filled with love. She covered Phronsie with kisses. "If you're a good girl, Phronsie, every day—that's the best present Santa could have."

"Then I'll be good always, Polly!"

On Christmas morning, Polly called upstairs, "Merry Christmas!"

Quick as a flash Joel, Davie, and Phronsie jumped out of their beds and headed straight for their stockings.

"Santa did come!" Phronsie yelled as she spun around, hugging her very full red stocking.

"Taffy!" Davie said, stuffing a piece into his mouth.

"Oh, Davie! Candy for breakfast?" Mrs. Pepper exclaimed with a smile.

"Candy's the best breakfast!" Joel added, munching on his own piece.

The three little Peppers emptied their stockings. They laughed and smiled over each and every gift.

"I wish every day was Christmas," Joel said, tooting on the whistle Ben had made him.

"It can't always be Christmas, Joel," Mrs. Pepper answered him with a smile.

"When can we light the tree?" Polly asked in a whisper.

"Mamsie said she would do it," Ben whispered back.

"Is your Santa costume safe?" Polly said.

"Tucked away. They would never find it," Ben chuckled.

"I wish Jasper were here," Polly sighed.

By five o'clock that evening, everyone was tired from the excitement of the day. Meanwhile, Mrs. Pepper had been busy in her own way. She came into the kitchen and set down her candle on the table. She gave Ben a secret nod, and he quietly slipped out of the room.

"Now, children," Mrs. Pepper said. "I want you to come with me."

Mrs. Pepper and Polly moved the children toward the storage room.

"Mamsie, why are we going in there?" Joel complained.

Just then, Mamsie swung open the door. The children's eyes opened wide. With a gasp, they ran into the storage room.

Polly took one look and sank right down to the floor.

"It's a fairyland!" Joel cried.

The whole room was buzzing with chatter and fun. In the center of it all was the most beautiful tree that Polly had ever seen. It was ablaze with candles. On its branches were beautiful ornaments and delicious-looking treats. A pile of presents glittered below it. And, standing around the tree were all their good friends in Badgertown: Mrs. Henderson and the parson, Dr. Fisher, and Grandma Bascom.

Suddenly there was a rattle at the window.

"It's Santa Claus!" Phronsie, Joel, and Davie shrieked.

In jumped a little, old man with a jolly, red

face and a pack on his back. Instead of wishing everyone a "Merry Christmas," he ran over to Mrs. Pepper and asked with surprise, "Mamsie, how did you do it?"

"It's Ben!" Phronsie shouted.

Ben grabbed Polly's hands and joyfully spun her around in circles.

All of the Peppers joined in, shouting and laughing along.

"Hold on there!" Parson Henderson shouted above the din. "I have a letter here for Santa," he said.

Ben took the letter and read it aloud:

Dear Mrs. Pepper, Polly, Ben, Phronsie, Joel, and Davie,

Merry Christmas to you all! I hope you'll have a good time. Please enjoy this Christmas as much as I've enjoyed my good times at your house. See you this summer, with my sister and all of my nephews in tow!

Your friend,
Jasper Elyot King

Dr. Fisher picked up a present marked with a big card that said, FOR MISS POLLY PEPPER, TO GIVE HER MUSIC EVERY DAY OF THE YEAR, FROM JASPER, and handed it to her.

It was a lovely brass cage. In it was a dear little bird with two bright black eyes that looked straight into Polly's merry brown ones. Polly burst into tears.

"I never thought I'd have a bird of my very own!" she exclaimed.

Gifts came flying fast after that. Ben got a new suit of clothes that fit him perfectly. A shawl fell down on Mrs. Pepper's shoulders. A work-basket and a cookbook tumbled into Polly's lap.

Tops and balls and fishing poles sent Joel and Davie into a corner, howling with delight. There were books and brightly wrapped candy boxes for everyone.

There was also a big doll dressed in a pink silk dress with a note that read, FOR PHRONSIE, FROM THE ONE WHO ENJOYED HER GINGERBREAD BOY.

The best present of all was for Polly. It was a plant stand containing dozens of different flowerpots with flowers enough to blossom for the whole year.

From the corner of the room, Joel's voice piped up, "You said it couldn't always be Christmas, Mamsie." Then he looked around at all the treasures and the happy, shining faces. "But I think it will be Christmas forever!"

CHAPTER 11

Polly Takes a Trip

⌒∽

The Peppers tried their hardest to figure out a way to thank Jasper and his father for what they had done. Ben and the little boys sent handmade boxes and carvings. Polly and Phronsie baked little cakes and decorated them with Polly's flowers. All winter, letters filled with messages from the Peppers and news from Jasper flew back and forth between the two houses.

"There's just no way to thank him properly, Mamsie," Polly said, with her bird Cherry perched on her shoulder. "I can hardly wait till summer when Jasper comes back."

"Write him a letter all by yourself and tell him so, Polly," Mrs. Pepper said.

"Jasper and Ben write ever so much better than I do, Mamsie," Polly worried.

"Well, someday soon we'll have enough money to send Ben to a proper school. Then we'll save up some more and send you, too," Mrs. Pepper vowed, bending her head over her sewing.

Polly was quiet.

"What's wrong, Polly?" Mrs. Pepper asked, looking up from her work.

"Well, if Ben goes to school and learns about everything first—will he be ashamed of me because of all the things I don't know?" Polly asked slowly, her lips trembling.

"Of course not, Polly, dear," Mrs. Pepper said, biting off a loose thread.

Then Mrs. Pepper returned to her sewing with great energy, as if the faster she sewed, the faster Polly would be able to go to proper school with Ben.

Meanwhile, at Jasper's house, things were in an uproar. Jasper, his older sister Marian, and her sons, Van, Percy, and Dick, were pleading with Mr. King to arrange their summer plans. Jasper had told sister and his nephews all about Polly and the rest of the Peppers. They were as eager to meet the Peppers as Jasper was to see them again.

"I simply do not want to go anywhere this summer," Mr. King grumbled. "We have a perfectly lovely home, and I should like to stay and enjoy it," he said.

Jasper looked so sad, that kindhearted Marian felt she had to do something. "Why not invite one of the children to stay with us?" she suggested. "How about Ben?"

"I want Polly," Jasper pouted. He sounded just

like Phronsie when Jasper and Prince rescued her from the nasty organ man.

"Father? May Polly Pepper come to stay with us a while?" Jasper asked.

Mr. King looked sharply down his nose over his eyeglasses at Jasper. He was surprised at how pale and thin the boy looked. Perhaps it might do him some good to have the girl here, Mr. King thought to himself.

"Please, Father?" Jasper begged.

Grumbling, Mr. King set aside his newspaper and said, "Fine. We'll send for the girl. I'll write the letter to Mrs. Pepper myself. Tell Thomas he can take the letter with the afternoon mail."

Mr. King set about writing a long letter. In it, he outlined a plan for Polly to live with the Kings for the whole school year and get an education. There would be music lessons, French lessons, reading, writing, and math lessons. Polly would receive everything that Mr. King provided for his very own son. Three-quarters of an hour later, the letter was ready.

But, Polly didn't come! A polite letter of thanks from Mrs. Pepper did. In the letter, Mrs. Pepper stiffly explained that she could not accept such an enormous favor.

Mr. King stormed and fussed, begged and pleaded. Kind-hearted Marian sent her own gentle letter to Mrs. Pepper. Still she would not let Polly come.

It was only when Mr. King wrote that Jasper was in failing health and that only Polly could cheer him up that Mrs. Pepper agreed that Polly really must go. Now it was her turn to help Jasper.

 و

The news that Polly was moving to a big city spread quickly through Badgertown.

On the day Polly was supposed to leave, all her good friends were there to help load her trunk onto the stagecoach and see her off. Everyone was happy for her. Everyone except Polly herself!

When the time came to go, Polly burst into tears.

"I can't," Polly said, trembling and pale. "I can't leave Mamsie with all the work."

"But don't you see, dear," Mrs. Henderson said kindly, taking Polly aside. "You will be helping your mother twice as much if you get a good education."

"Oh, Polly, if you give this up, there will never be another chance," Ben said, his voice choked with tears.

"But it isn't right," Polly said.

Finally, Mrs. Pepper spoke up. She put her hands on Polly's shoulders. There was a look on her face that Polly had never seen before.

"Polly, my dear, if you don't go and learn as

much as you possibly can, I think my heart will break," Mrs. Pepper said. Then, to everyone's surprise, Mrs. Pepper burst out crying, right in front of everyone.

"Oh, Mamsie. Don't cry. If you think I should go—if you want me to go, then I will. I will," Polly said, flinging her arms around her mother. "But, I shall miss you so," Polly whispered, burying her head in her mother's neck.

"And, I will miss you," Mrs. Pepper whispered back. "Now we must be brave for the others," she added.

Mrs. Pepper wiped away Polly's tears and fixed Polly's hat. Everyone kissed and hugged Polly good-bye once again.

Just then, Joel cried out, "The stagecoach! It's leaving with your trunk on it, Polly!"

Sure enough, the coach was starting up. Quickly Polly climbed into the coach with the bags and bundles and boxes that wouldn't fit into her trunk. The coach rumbled its way to the train that would take her to the big city.

Somehow Polly and her bundles made it onto the train on time. Polly had never been on a train before. She took in every detail so she could tell Ben and the others what it was like. Looking out the window, she saw the countryside disappear into the distance. The thought of her family and the Little Brown House tugged at her heart. Polly cheered herself with knowing that now she was really doing something big to help her mother.

When the train arrived in the city station, all the passengers poured out of the train car. Polly just sat there. She wasn't quite sure what to do next.

"There she is!" shouted Mr. King from the train platform. He waved for the train conductor to help Polly off the train. In an instant, Polly, her trunk, and her bundles and boxes were delivered onto the platform in front of Jasper and

Mr. King. Soon Polly was settled into Mr. King's grand coach, comfortably sandwiched between Jasper and his father.

The coach flew through the heart of the city, on narrow, noisy, busy streets, and out into wide avenues with great handsome homes on either side. Then the coach turned in at a gate and drove up a tree-lined driveway to a beautiful house that

seemed like one of the castles in Ben's bedtime stories.

"Oh my goodness," said Polly, blushing very hard. "It's so lovely. Do you really live here?" she asked.

"We do. And now, so do you!" Jasper said with a laugh.

CHAPTER 12

A Warm Welcome

Mr. King helped Polly out of the coach and up the steps. Jasper followed with Polly's trunk. A stiff butler opened the door. Polly felt as if she'd floated away to the fairyland of her dreams. Before her were warm greetings, large rooms, and high walls decorated with elegant paintings.

Mr. King held her hand as though she were a fragile package. Jasper bobbed around, introducing her to his nephews, Van, Percy, and Dick. Jasper's dog Prince jumped up and down trying to lick her face. Best of all was when Jasper's beautiful and kind older sister, Marian, smiled into Polly's upturned face and welcomed her with a hug and a kiss.

"I am so very glad to have you here, Polly Pepper," Marian declared.

From that moment on, Polly knew she would always love Marian.

Marian took Polly's hand, "Come dear. I'll show you your room."

"We want to see her. Let Polly stay and play!" Van, Percy, and Dick cried.

"There's plenty of time for you to spend with Polly," Marian insisted, leading Polly up a wide oak staircase.

Polly clung for dear life to Marian's soft, white hand as she led Polly down a lovely, long hallway.

"Now Polly, I'm going to put you here in the room right next to mine. I hope you will be very happy in it." Then, because she couldn't help it, Marian hugged the scared, little Polly in her arms.

At dinner that night, all the boys chattered and laughed. They each had to tell Polly their stories. Polly described Ben and how much he liked to do woodwork. She explained about Phronsie and her adorable ways, and how Joel and Davie always made everyone laugh.

By the end of the evening, it seemed as though Polly had always lived there. As they left the table, Dick rushed up to Polly and flung himself into her arms.

"I love you!" Dick declared.

Nothing more was needed to make Polly feel at home.

~

Each day, Polly awoke eager to learn as much as she could—for Mamsie. She carefully studied her school subjects and worked very hard at learning French. Most of all, Polly looked forward to her daily piano lessons.

Polly loved the big piano in the drawing room. She barely noticed the shaded light, draped furniture, and thick, soft carpet. Polly only had eyes for the piano. Her music teacher was a funny, little man. Polly believed he was the magician who would unlock the secrets and mysteries of the piano. She admired him very much.

The music teacher was charmed by Polly. He was very impressed with the way Polly devoted herself to her music lessons and how she practiced every day before he arrived.

"I think Polly plays the piano better than any of us," Jasper announced proudly at dinner one evening.

"Polly is always practicing," Van said in a grumpy tone.

"She never has time to play with us," Percy added.

"I want Polly to play with me," Dick said.

"Leave Polly alone," Jasper said sternly.

"You think because you're thirteen you can tell us what to do," Van said. "But that's only three years older than I. So you can't tell me what to do, even if you are my uncle."

Polly had never heard such angry talk at the Little Brown House.

"Let's tell stories," Polly said in a bright voice. "We'll each tell one," she suggested.

"You tell us a story, Polly. You tell the best stories," the little boys begged.

So, Polly began one of her finest and funniest stories, which soon had all four boys giggling. Even Mr. King joined the fun.

"How do you think of things like that, Polly Pepper?" Van asked, his face red from laughing.

"That isn't anything compared to the stories she used to tell at the Little Brown House," Jasper exclaimed.

Jasper noticed Polly's face. At the mention of the Little Brown House, Polly had turned pale, and her brown eyes drooped. Her sad little face went right to Jasper's heart. Could Polly be homesick already?

That night, and every night, when no one could see, tears would roll down Polly's rosy cheeks. The only place in the King house where Polly was truly happy, other than in front of the piano, was in the family greenhouse. After schoolwork, piano practice, and telling stories to the boys, Polly would rush to the greenhouse where old Turner, the gardener, tended the flowers.

But even with the music and the flowers, the light in Polly's merry brown eyes was never very bright. She grew more silent and pale and droopy with each passing day.

Mr. King decided to take matters into his own hands to solve the problem. One day, he simply said he was going out for a very long ride. He wouldn't be home for lunch, and they should eat without him.

That same day, while Polly was practicing piano, she was also wishing she could see Phronsie—just for a moment. Knowing she couldn't was almost more than she could bear.

Just then, Polly heard a little voice cry out, "Where is she? Where's Polly?" Thinking she had imagined it, Polly shook her head to clear her thoughts. But, in the twinkle of an eye, a little, yellow head popped up on the other side of the piano. "Here I am, Polly. I'm here!" Phronsie cried.

Polly was so surprised she couldn't speak. If Jasper hadn't caught her, she would have tumbled backward off the stool.

"Aren't you glad I've come, Polly?" Phronsie

asked, climbing into her lap and putting her little face close to Polly's.

Polly hugged Phronsie close and buried her face in Phronsie's yellow hair.

Mr. King, Jasper, and his sister, Marian, looked on and smiled. Jasper's nephews were so excited they could hardly stand it.

For the first time in a long time, Polly's heart was glad.

CHAPTER 13

Phronsie's Big Adventure

❦

Phronsie settled right into life at the Kings's household. But each day, while Polly, Jasper, and the boys had their lessons, Phronsie had no one to play with. So, Mr. King made sure that Phronsie had a new doll each day.

One day while Phronsie played tea party in the far corner of Marian's bedroom, Polly rushed in, waving a letter in the air. Phronsie overheard Polly say that she had forgotten to give Thomas, Mr. King's butler, her weekly letter to the Little Brown House to take to the post office.

"Mamsie will be so disappointed, I can't bear it," Polly cried.

"We'll send out the letter tomorrow, my dear," Marian said, putting down her sewing.

"But she'll be expecting it tomorrow," Polly said, practically in tears.

"Now, Polly, your mother wouldn't want you to be upset and miss your piano lesson over this. Leave the letter in the hallway, and Thomas will take it into town tomorrow for the morning mail," Marian said, comforting Polly.

"I guess I must," Polly said, leaving to meet her music teacher in the drawing room for her piano lesson.

Marian returned to her sewing. A thoughtful expression came over Phronsie's face. She kissed each of her dolls good-bye and pattered out the hallway and down the stairs. There, she found the letter to Mamsie that Polly had been holding.

"Mamsie will feel so bad when she doesn't get

Polly's letter. I know the way to the post office. I've been there with Grandpa King," Phronsie said to herself.

Phronsie picked up the letter and slipped out the door. Nobody saw the little girl going down the driveway. At the gate, she looked up and down the street trying to remember which way she had gone with Grandpa King.

Phronsie started out and immediately turned down the wrong street, but she continued on and on, carefully holding the letter from Polly.

At last, Phronsie reached the main street. She didn't come to the post office, so she kept on going. Phronsie kept turning, corner after corner, ducking out of the way of the crowds of people who were walking up and down the street. A woman carrying a big basket bumped into Phronsie. She knocked off Phronsie's bonnet, sending it into the middle of the coach-filled street.

Without thinking, Phronsie ran into the middle of the road to get her bonnet.

"Look out!" someone called. "Stop!" shouted another.

The crowd gasped as a powerful pair of horses, whose driver could not stop them in time, came racing along the street, straight toward Phronsie.

"The little girl will be killed!" cried someone from the crowd.

Phronsie sprang between the horses' hooves and reached the curb on the other side of the street just in time! Phronsie fell into a crowd of men.

"What's this?" asked a man as Phronsie bumped against him.

"That was a narrow escape! This little girl was nearly killed a moment ago—careless driving," said another.

"Bless me!" said a third. "Phronsie, is that you?" asked Mr. King. His face went deathly pale.

"Grandpa!" Phronsie cried out.

Without another word, Mr. King scooped up Phronsie into his strong arms as if he would never let her go.

"What in heaven's name are you doing here, child?" Mr. King asked.

Phronsie explained about Polly's letter to Mamsie. Mr. King shuddered at the thought of what could have happened to Phronsie.

"Well, I'll make sure that Mamsie gets her letter, my child. Let's get you home safe and sound, now," Mr. King said tenderly, as he hailed a coach.

When Mr. King arrived home with Phronsie, no one had realized she was gone!

"How could this have happened?" Mr. King roared. He explained about Phronsie's near-escape under the hooves of the horses.

Polly grew pale at the thought. She held Phronsie close in her lap.

"I don't care about doing lessons. I'll never let you out of my sight again," Polly promised.

"It's okay, Polly," Phronsie said, patting Polly's cheek. "Mamsie will get her letter. You'll see. Grandpa will take care of it."

"Oh, Phronsie!" Polly cried, hugging her tight.

Mr. King realized how much both little girls needed and missed their mother. So, Mr. King came up with another plan, and he wrote it in a letter to Mrs. Pepper.

⌒

Several nights later, when the rest of the house was asleep, Phronsie woke up suddenly. She heard a noise downstairs.

"Grandpa!" Phronsie thought to herself. "I want to see Grandpa."

Phronsie climbed out of bed and with her little feet bare, slowly tiptoed down the wide, oak staircase. She saw a light coming from Grandpa's library.

"I'll surprise him!" Phronsie thought happily. Her soft feet pattered over the thick carpet. She stood at the library doorway. Then she stopped perfectly still.

Two men were taking things out of Grandpa's writing desk and putting them into a great big sack.

"What are you doing with my grandpa's things?" Phronsie asked.

The two masked men stared with surprise at the little girl, too shocked to move.

Phronsie took a step into the library. "Don't touch my dear grandpa's things!"

Suddenly a deep growl and rush of fur flew past Phronsie, heading straight for the burglars.

"Yikes! Let's get out of here!" cried one.

The burglars dropped the sack filled with Mr. King's things, leaped out the window, and ran across the long lawn, Prince chasing behind them.

"Polly! Grandpa!" Phronsie called.

Polly, followed by Mr. King, Marian, Jasper, and his nephews, rushed down the stairs to find Phronsie in the library in the middle of the clutter of Mr. King's belongings.

"Whatever is going on?" Mr. King asked, scooping Phronsie up in his arms.

"Some bad men were taking your things, Grandpa!" Phronsie said, shaking her head. "Prince chased them away!" she added.

Just then, Prince returned to the room, panting and tired.

"Good dog," Jasper said, patting his head and scratching Prince between the ears.

"Oh my," Polly said, realizing the danger Phronsie had been in.

Then before anyone could say anything, Polly fainted away onto the floor.

CHAPTER 14

A Surprise for Polly and Phronsie

⟍ᑳ

That night, Phronsie refused to sleep anywhere but with Polly.

The next morning, while Polly and Phronsie slept through breakfast, there was a lot of activity in the King residence. Mr. King had a special surprise for the two little Pepper girls. Marian, Jasper, and the nephews could barely contain their excitement. After breakfast, Mr. King and Marian rode off in their coach.

"We'll be back soon," they told the boys. "Remember, Jasper, don't tell Polly or Phronsie a thing, or you'll spoil the surprise," Mr. King warned.

Many hours passed. The boys could not sit still.

"Is it time yet?" asked Van, the oldest of Jasper's nephews.

"Are they back yet?" asked Percy, squirming in his seat with anticipation.

"Will Polly still play with us and tell us stories?" asked Dick with a worried expression.

"Everything will be exactly the same, only better!" Jasper assured them.

Suddenly, all four boys heard the sound of a coach approaching.

Van, Percy, and Dick ran to Jasper's side. "Is it them?" the boys cried in unison.

But, the coach passed the King home and kept on going down the street.

Polly and Phronsie appeared hand-in-hand, their faces still flushed with sleep.

"Is it who?" Polly asked with a yawn.

"Where's Grandpa?" Phronsie wanted to know.

Just then, a coach drove through the brick gateway and right up to the house.

"They're here!" Jasper cried.

All four boys raced to the door, each one wanting to be the first to open it. Polly and Phronsie followed, confused by all the fuss.

Then, the front door opened. Mr. King and Marian stood on either side of the doorway.

"Here we are!" Mr. King said with a sweep of his hand.

Much to Polly's and Phronsie's surprise, there, at their very door, stood Mamsie, Ben, Joel, and Davie!

Polly rubbed her eyes as though she couldn't believe what she was seeing.

"Mamsie!" Phronsie shrieked and flung herself into Mamsie's waiting arms.

At the same time, Ben, Joel, and Davie cried out, "Polly!"

They rushed to put their arms around her as though it had been a hundred years since they had seen her last. It almost felt like it had.

From that day on, all of the Peppers lived at the King home. To show her thanks for all Mr. King had done for them, Mrs. Pepper offered to help Mr. King by taking care of the household duties. Mr. King happily agreed.

In this way, Ben and Polly and Jasper would all have their lessons together everyday. Ben would have special art lessons, for he was quite talented in both painting and drawing. Polly would continue with her music lessons, and the three littlest Peppers would go to school with Van, Percy, and Dick.

Polly and Ben told stories every night, and laughter filled the King home, just as it had for so many years in the Little Brown House.

What Do *You* Think?
Questions for Discussion

⌒↻

Have you ever been around a toddler who keeps asking the question "Why?" all the time? Does your teacher call on you in class with questions from your homework? Do your parents ask you questions about your day at the dinner table? We are always surrounded by questions that need a specific response. But is it possible to have a question with no right answer?

The following questions are about the book you just read. But this is not a quiz! They are designed to help you look at the people, places, and events in the story from different angles. These questions do not have specific answers. Instead, they might make you think of the story in a completely new way.

Think carefully about each question and enjoy discovering more about this classic story.

1. What do the Pepper children call their mother? Do you have a nickname for either of your parents?

2. How do each of the children help out around the house? Do you have any chores?

3. How do the Pepper children decide to surprise Mamsie for her birthday? Have you ever planned a surprise for someone? Did it work?

4. Ben says the best meal would be roast beef, potatoes, and pie. If you could pick your food for any meal, what would you choose?

5. When Phronsie and Ben come down with

the measles, they have to stay in bed. Have you ever been that sick? How did it make you feel?

6. Why do you suppose the Peppers' neighbors help them so much? Have you ever helped someone in need?

7. How does Mr. King respond to Phronsie's gingerbread boy? What is the most thoughtful gift you've ever received?

8. How does Polly feel when she goes to stay with the Kings? Have you ever been homesick? How did you get over it?

9. Mr. King at first seems to be tough and mean, but in fact he is quite kind. Have you ever met anyone like him?

10. The Pepper children are similar in many ways, but they are also quite different. How do they differ from each other? Which Pepper are you the most like?

Afterword

By Arthur Pober, Ed.D.

❧

First impressions are important.

Whether we are meeting new people, going to new places, or picking up a book unknown to us, first impressions count for a lot. They can lead to warm, lasting memories or can make us shy away from any future encounters.

Can you recall your own first impressions and earliest memories of reading the classics?

Do you remember wading through pages and pages of text to prepare for an exam? Or were you the child who hid under the blanket to read with a flashlight, joining forces with Robin Hood to save Maid Marian? Do you remember only how long it took you to read a lengthy novel such as *Little Women*? Or did you become best friends with the March sisters?

Even for a gifted young reader, getting through long chapters with dense language can easily become overwhelming and can obscure the richness of the story and its characters. Reading an abridged, newly crafted version of a classic novel can be the gentle introduction a child needs to explore the characters and storyline without the frustration of difficult vocabulary and complex themes.

Reading an abridged version of a classic novel gives the young reader a sense of independence and the satisfaction of finishing a "grown-up" book. And when a child is engaged with and inspired by a classic story, the tone is set for further exploration of the story's themes, characters, history, and details. As a child's reading skills advance, the desire to tackle the original, unabridged version of the story will naturally emerge.

If made accessible to young readers, these stories can become invaluable tools for understanding themselves in the context of their families and social environments. This is why the Classic Starts series includes questions that stimulate discussion regarding the impact and social relevance of the characters and stories today. These questions can foster lively conversations between children and their parents or teachers. When we look at the issues, values, and standards of past times in terms of how we live now, we can appreciate literature's classic tales in a very personal and engaging way.

Share your love of reading the classics with a young child, and introduce an imaginary world real enough to last a lifetime.

Dr. Arthur Pober, Ed.D.

Dr. Arthur Pober has spent more than twenty years in the fields of early childhood and gifted education. He is the former principal of one of the world's oldest laboratory schools for gifted youngsters, Hunter College Elementary School, and former Director of Magnet Schools for the Gifted and Talented for more than 25,000 youngsters in New York City.

Dr. Pober is a recognized authority in the areas of media and child protection and is currently the U.S. representative to the European Institute for the Media and European Advertising Standards Alliance.

Explore these wonderful stories in our
Classic Starts™ library.